SURPRISINGLY

sarah

SURPRISINGLY

sarah

TERRI LIBENSON

BALZER + BRAY
An Imprint of HarperCollinsPublishers

Balzer + Bray is an imprint of HarperCollins Publishers.

Surprisingly Sarah
Copyright © 2023 by Terri Libenson
All rights reserved. Printed in the United States of America.
No part of this book may be used or reproduced in any manner whatsoever without
written permission except in the case of brief quotations embodied in critical articles
and reviews. For information address HarperCollins Children's Books, a division of
HarperCollins Publishers, 195 Broadway, New York, NY 10007.
www.harpercollinschildrens.com

Library of Congress Control Number: 2022949256
ISBN 978-0-06-313922-0 (hardcover) — ISBN 978-0-06-313921-3 (pbk.) —
ISBN 978-0-06-332344-5 (special ed.)

Typography by Terri Libenson and Laura Mock
23 24 25 26 27 PC/WOR 10 9 8 7 6 5 4 3 2 1

First Edition

To Michael:
I think I chose well.

PROLOGUE
SARAH

You know that girl in the cafeteria who's surrounded by a ton of friends? Whose phone always blows up with texts? Who goes to parties every weekend?

Well, that's not me.

I don't really have a lot of friends—but I don't mind. I'd rather have a few close friends than a big group of not-so-close ones. Also, the ones I **do** have, I hold on to tight (specifically, three of them). Maybe it's because I see so many kids at school go through friends like paper towels. They use them, crumple them up, and move on to others.

I feel the same way about other things: hobbies, books, stuffed animals. I have a small bunch that I love and stay loyal to. But, other than family, my close friends are the most important thing to me.

I have one oldest friend ("old" as in longtime, not "old-old"). His name is Leo Catalino (I love how that flows!), and he lives right next door to me. We've been neighbors forever and best friends practically since we were born.

Leo is in seventh grade like me. He loves being outside . . . a lot. I do, too, but not as much as he does. He likes to play basketball or Hacky Sack in his driveway. I usually sit on my stoop and draw fabric patterns and clothing designs while we talk and shout to each other. Sometimes he'll take a break, sit on the steps, and eat snacks with me.

Our houses aren't big, and they're pretty old, but they do have large covered front porches. We like to hang out on mine because it's so cute and homey. My mom decorated it with plants and flowerpots, little wood chairs, a small table, and a multicolor outdoor rug. Leo and I like to play Bananagrams on the rug or sit on the steps, talk, and people watch. But the best thing?

nature show

safety of porch

My mom isn't thrilled that the porch has turned into:

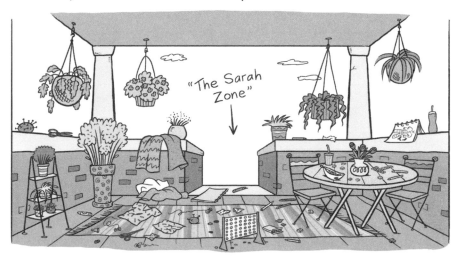

"The Sarah Zone"

But as much as she grumbles, I think she's secretly happy I use that space. Especially when Leo is around. She loves Leo.

forkful of pie

how she shows her affection

Today, we're not on the porch because we have school. The good news is we can walk to the bus stop together. The bad news is Leo goes to a different school. So when we get to my stop, I stay there and he keeps walking. He goes to a private school, Ellings Way. (He likes to sound out its initials, "EW," which used to make me giggle.) Ellings is really big, really old, and really pretty.

I hate it.

Leo would rather go to school at Lakefront Middle with me and some of his other elementary school friends, like Ben Friedman. But Leo's parents think EW is better and will "pave the way for college." I get it. They want the best for him. He doesn't want to disappoint them, so he feels kinda:

It's a warm day in May, my favorite month. We're walking to my stop while eating homemade breakfast burritos (my mom made a huge batch—Leo's favorites).

There's already a bunch of kids at the bus stop. Everyone's in shorts and tees and talking a lot. I love that it's spring. The big school dance is coming up. If there's anything I like almost as much as warm weather and designing clothes, it's dancing. I used to take hip-hop and Mexican folk until I realized I liked making my costumes more than being in recitals.

He gives me a weird look.

That's what we call each other: BGF for Best Girl Friend (not girlfriend) and BBF for Best Boy Friend (definitely not boyfriend).

The bus pulls up and I get on. I wave at Leo through the window as he walks. There's guacamole on his backpack. No idea how it got there, but that's pretty typical.

When I get to school, I see Ben right away.

Here's the thing. I have a massive crush on Ben. Every time I see him, I feel like I'm a victim of a horrible-yet-dreamy disease.

symptoms of the Ben-bonic Plague:

muddled brain →

cold sweat

pounding heart →

shakes

fever →

urge to embrace my inflicter

I didn't always feel this way. But about a year ago, some

seismic shift took place in my heart and now here we are.

I take a deep breath and walk over.

Joe Lungo and I have weirdly become almost . . . well, I wouldn't say **friends** or anything. But definitely friendlier. Ever since the Student Showcase. That was a great night. I won the comics contest and then we went to Taystee's in a big group and had so much fun.

Ever since then, Joe says hi to me in the halls and calls me

"Lass" (his nickname because of a jumper I wear, which looks like a kilt). But he actually treats me like a human being now instead of teasing me or acting out.

I think it's because I treat him like a human being, too. I guess that's the solution. I should tell the others.

He jigs away.

I try to clear my head. I take another deep breath (my friend Emmie's mom calls this a "cleansing breath deep from your root chakra") and start walking slowly toward Ben. I'm both relieved and terrified that he's still there. And still alone.

Before I can think, he slams his locker door shut and I jump.

He opens his locker again and pulls out something from the top shelf. His gym shoes fly out. They just miss his head. He hands me a small black earbud case with a fuzzy—and peeling—burger emoji sticker. Leo loves burgers.

Ben quickly bends down to pick up his stinky-looking shoes while I stand there. My hands are getting sweaty, and my feet feel like cinder blocks. I can't move.

My hands are all shaky and clammy. Does he notice? OMG, I should've worn a cotton shirt, not this nylon one. I'm sweating right through it. And I did such a bad job stitching the hem. What was I thinking . . . ?

Okay, never mind that.

I take one last deep, shaky breath.

And then . . .

Should I be really brave and ask Ben to the spring dance?

Or not?

What do you think I should do?

'Cause I don't know if he likes me back, and I don't wanna get rejected.

SARAH

I take one last deep, shaky breath.
And then . . .

Ben looks like I hit him in the head with a bag of rubber chickens. (I once saw that in a cartoon and the character had the same expression.)

He turns bright red and quickly looks toward his left, down the hall. It's not that crowded yet. Then he looks at his feet. Converses. Or maybe the fake ones.

Meanwhile . . .

I exhale. I realize I was holding my breath for a long time. It comes out in one long

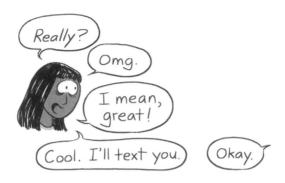

I rush away, smiling and waving. He waves back.

sort of

I try and keep it together until I round the corner. Then I see Emmie and Brianna.

squeeeeeeal

We all squeal loudly until I see Ben and his friends head down the hall.

I'm squeezing Bri's arm in excitement without realizing it. She clears her throat, and I let go. I forgot she's not the touchy-feely type. I'm the total opposite, but I'm really trying to respect boundaries. We learned all about that in Health. Mr. Bauman also taught us about consent. It was kinda eye-opening for a girl who likes to express herself by squeezing arms, grabbing hands, and giving atomic hugs. Emmie's shyer than me (like with a capital S), but she doesn't mind.

squeeeze SQUEAK

human security blanket... ← and squeaky toy

Leo's like me. Everyone thinks we're boyfriend and girlfriend because we're always hugging and holding hands, but it's just how we are. We're family.

Maybe we can help decorate for the dance. I saw a flyer for that.

Yeah!!

That'd be cool.

I'm the world's worst artist, but I'm pretty good at ordering people around.

You don't say.

We all walk to our homerooms together. I feel like the luckiest girl alive. I've got my best friend, Leo. And in the past few months, I've gotten really close with Em and Bri (although it took a while for Bri to warm up to me). And they are the most loyal friends ever. And now I'm going to the dance with Ben Friedman, the boy I've crushed on for a year!

Only . . .

Leo knows nothing about my crush. At least I don't think so. I've never told him. And I have no idea how he'd react to my taking Ben—one of his closest friends—to the dance.

We all used to go to elementary school together. Me, Leo, and Ben. I never really talked much to Ben, though. I was scared of all boys except for Leo. I know that seems weird, but it's true.

I was raised only around women. My mom, of course. But I've also grown up with my aunt, Tía Elena, who's single, and my abuela (grandma). They live close by. My parents divorced when I was little. My dad lives in California, and I rarely see him. We talk only about once a year.

Leo's dads are really nice. They're probably the best examples I have of what fathers are like. They sometimes treat Leo and me to ice cream on weekends. But they work full-time, so I don't see a lot of them.

And as for Leo, he's more like a brother than a guy. So, yeah, I'm not exactly smooth around boys.

the time I lost all my vowels

I glide through the day in a great mood. I haven't seen Ben since this morning, but that's okay. I'm still floating from his answer.

After the bus drops me off, I walk home alone. My mom is already in the house, cooking up a storm. That's her passion. She makes the best food in the world. She also shares my love of clothes. She helps me with my patterns and designs. Together, we make the most amazing outfits.

fashion model vibes

Mamá works two jobs: her main one is as an executive assistant. But she also has a "side hustle" as a pastry chef. She makes desserts at home and delivers the orders by car—aka "Julia the Jalopy" (her oldish-but-reliable Toyota).

old car

Mamá Maricel's
Sweets 2 Go

new sign

We don't have a lot of money, but we don't really need much. My abuela gave us her house after my abuelo died (before I was born). It's roomy enough for two, and other than repairs (which my mom can do, too!), it's all paid for.

"M" for "Marvelous,"
"aMazing," and
"Masterful"
Mamá
(NEVER
"Mean" or
"Malicious")

My aunt and abuela live in a newer, one-story house nearby. Tía Elena is some kind of scientist (Mamá says she does research), and she takes care of my grandma, who can't work at all since she has really bad arthritis. I love visiting them. Tía Elena has a huge backyard screen for movies and a built-in firepit. In the warm months, we sit in her yard, watch movies together under blankets, and toast marshmallows. Leo joins us all the time. We like to chase fireflies around the yard, which makes my abuela laugh.

"Cachetona" means "chubby cheeked" in Spanish. When I was little, women used to grab my cheeks between their fingers and pinch **hard**. I'm scarred for life.

They're still kinda chubby. But I don't want to be reminded.

I tell her about Ben, and she squeals, too.

They are. I grab one.

She laughs while I run out the front door and grab my sketchbook and colored pencils off the porch table. I sit on the stoop and start drawing right away. I love it. I'm in art class and art club with Emmie and Tyler Ross. We all like to draw different things, though.

Reluctantly, I lower the sketchbook. There are a few small drawings of brightly colored, swingy dresses ("skater dresses"). I love the ones that swish around.

I put my sketchbook down.

He runs into his house to change and put away his backpack. I remember his earbuds and go inside to get them. Leo comes out in shorts and a striped T-shirt, with a big bag of chips tucked under his arm. We head through the rickety fence to his backyard and grab the little red and blue beanbags. Soon, we're playing the game, chomping on chips, and goofing around.

I'm glad he didn't ask me more about the dress designs. I don't know why I didn't tell him about Ben and the dance. He's gonna find out, anyway. If I don't say anything, Ben sure will.

text from Ben

NOOOOOOOOOO

vzzzz

panicked interception

I will tell him. Just not now. Not yet. But soon. Like after this game.

Or maybe tomorrow.

35

SHE SIGHS. I SCOOCH NEXT TO HER.

oww

bump

SHE STARTS TO SAY SOMETHING BUT HESITATES.

C'mon. It's me.

Okay...but this might be kind of a surprise to you.

I DON'T KNOW WHAT TO SAY.

Leo? Do you think he would have said yes? Like, do you think he'd like me back?

SHE LOOKS HOPEFUL AND SCARED AT THE SAME TIME. BUT I CAN'T LIE.

The only girl I know he liked was someone named Lindsay Donsky. He really liked the way she smelled.

But I guess she's taken.

SHE LOOKS CONFUSED.

It's a video g—Never mind.

WE'RE QUIET FOR A MOMENT.

bump

You can still ask him.

I already told Em and Bri I'd go with them. And we're all joining the decorating committee.

I'VE GOTTA SAY, EVEN THOUGH I'M SURPRISED, I SHOULDN'T BE. LAST SUMMER, THINGS STARTED GETTING WEIRD WHENEVER BEN CAME AROUND.

47

BEN NEVER SAID ANYTHING, BUT *I* WAS SURE GETTING FREAKED OUT. SARAH JUST WASN'T HERSELF.

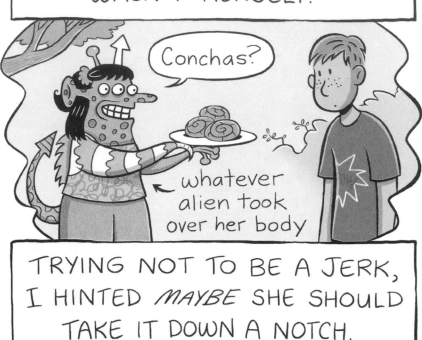

TRYING NOT TO BE A JERK, I HINTED *MAYBE* SHE SHOULD TAKE IT DOWN A NOTCH.

AFTER THAT, IT WAS JUST EASIER FOR ME TO GO TO BEN'S.

WHICH WAS FINE FOR A WHILE, EXCEPT:

IT WASN'T ALWAYS LIKE THIS. BEN USED TO LIKE DOING THE SAME STUFF AS ME.

BUT WHAT CAN I DO? NEXT TO SARAH, BEN'S MY OLDEST FRIEND. IT'S NOT LIKE I HAVE ANYONE AT SCHOOL.

I guess that's my own fault.

SARAH STILL LOOKS DEPRESSED. AND ALTHOUGH I'M KINDA MIFFED THAT SHE NEVER TOLD ME ABOUT HER THING FOR BEN...

...I REALLY, REALLY HATE IT WHEN SHE'S DOWN.

You know...

What?

I can go with you.

I told you... I'm going with Em and Bri.

Yeah, but they're not me. We love dancing. It's always fun. Remember the Half-Tilted Pigeon Waddle?

This isn't my room with my speaker blasting and the shades down. And if you did that at the dance, I'd murder you.

ha ha

Ha, okay.

SHE HUGS ME.
NOT SURPRISING.
SARAH'S A HUGGER.

But thank you.

Sure.

Yeah. Of course.

You'll keep this a secret, right?

WE PINKY SWEAR. SILLY, I KNOW, BUT IT MAKES HER FEEL BETTER.

You're the bestest BBF, Leo.

THAT SHOULD MAKE ME FEEL REALLY GOOD...

...SO I DON'T KNOW WHY IT DOESN'T.

SARAH

News travels fast.

A minute later, we're on my stoop. It's dark out. Our street isn't busy, so we can hear the usual chorus of crickets. And every so often, the low **wrrrrnnn** of a motorcycle pack on the highway.

I don't answer at first (which, I guess, is an answer in itself).

But for some reason, I don't want him to know about my crush. First, Leo could let it slip out accidentally. Second, I don't want to put him in the middle in case Ben doesn't like me back. Sure, Ben said yes to the dance, but maybe he was just being nice.*

And third? Actually, I don't know what the third reason is. It's there, but I can't name it.

*Either way, I still want to go with him. 'Cause there's always a chance that by the end of the dance, he **will** like me back!

I think I figured out the third reason. Leo would think I'm ridiculous, crushing on someone like Ben. Okay, so he's just a regular guy, not Mr. Popularity or anything, but he's still cooler than me.

Leo just stares at me.

unnerving

 Know what'd be fun? If you came, too, with one of my friends? Then we could all hang out!

Leo looks down and mutters:

 That's okay.

 Leo, do you want me to uninvite him? I know it's kinda weird because he's your friend and all....

It's fine.

secretly
relieved

Look, I've gotta go. I have a French test tomorrow and I suck at languages.

Before I can react, he's already running up his porch steps.

See you tomorrow, BBF?

He doesn't smile. He just gives me a little wave and goes inside.

It's not the first time Leo's been upset with me. We've had lots of fights, usually about stupid things.

But this is the first time I don't know the **reason** he's upset with me. Is it 'cause I didn't tell him about asking Ben to the dance? Or 'cause he thinks I'm stealing his friend behind his back? Or that I'd want to hang out with Ben over him?

I go back inside and plop down on my abuelo's old recliner. It's comfy and comforting. I don't know what my grandfather actually smelled like, but the chair has a faint aroma.

Mamá said he was an avid outdoorsperson. I wish I had known him.

liked fishing and hiking

had my eyes (or vice versa)

loved giving Abuela surprises from nature, like flowers and dead fish

Are boys really so complicated? At least I know where I stand with my dad (nowhere). I could always count on Leo, but I went and messed it up, and now I don't know what he's thinking.

Only thing I do know is:

He needs to cool off.

That's it! He just needs to chill and then he'll come around again. He always does.

I'm baaaack!

I heave myself off the plushy chair and head to the kitchen. Mamá is cooling more donuts.

She shoots me a look while I nibble.

It's so hard to hide my feelings. Tía Elena calls my face "expressive." But it's my downfall. I can't hide anything.

Picasso
← face

← every
expression
at once

I'm just tired. I don't have homework, so I think I'll go to bed.

I'm surprised you're not drawing more dress designs.

Yeah. Leo squashed my enthusiasm. Guess I need some cooling off, too.

I head upstairs. Em and Bri love my bedroom because there's a crawl space in one of the walls. It's practically a whole other room! There's just enough space to sit in (even though I've bumped my head on the ceiling more times than I can remember). I strung up fairy lights and keep my small collection of graphic novels and old stuffed animals in there. I also tacked colorful fabric to the walls. Emmie and Bri have even added their own touches.

Bri's glow-in-the-dark stickers

Emmie's drawings

We use it as a little clubhouse. My mom can't hear us in there, so we can talk as loud as we want. I think I've lost count of how many times I've giggled about Ben or Emmie's gushed about Tyler or Bri's rolled her eyes at us.

Leo won't go in there because he's claustrophobic. That's probably why he loves being outside. It's too bad . . . but then again, it's nice to have a space just for my "newer" friends and me.

I don't go in there right now. Instead, I flop on my beanbag and text Emmie.

I hesitate.

We text for another minute. Then I plug in my phone in the hallway (Mamá's strict) and get ready for bed. But before I crawl under the covers, I decide to tiptoe back in the hall to check my phone one last time. Leo usually sends me funny videos or memes at night.

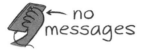
← no messages

I have a hard time falling asleep. I can't stand it when anyone's upset with me. Especially when I don't know why. I don't like leaving things . . . um . . .

"Unresolved"
Winn Word of the week
← English teacher

Or "hanging in the air," as Leo once called it when his parents had a fight and didn't speak for two days. He practically lived at my house to get away from the tension.

But I finally do fall asleep.

Because here's the last thing I remember before drifting off: despite the stuff that's hanging in the air . . .

. . . I'm sure we'll be okay.

Leo She lost her nerve

I'M SITTING IN MY LAST CLASS OF THE DAY: FRENCH (BOO).

I CAN'T STOP THINKING ABOUT YESTERDAY.

TRUTH IS, OTHER THAN BEING KINDA ANNOYED BY HER, BEN BARELY KNOWS SARAH EXISTS.

BUT I CAN'T TELL HER THAT. IT'LL CRUSH HER.

AND I KNOW A THING OR TWO ABOUT CRUSHES.

BUT EVEN WHEN AVA MOVED TO TEXAS LAST YEAR...

SARAH FINALLY CONVINCED ME TO REMOVE AVA FROM MY SNAPGAB. THAT HELPED...

AND I'LL SAY ONE THING ABOUT STARTING EW. I WAS SO DISTRACTED (AND MAD AT MY PARENTS)...

MAYBE WHAT _I_ NEED TO DO IS DISTRACT SARAH FROM BEN. TO HELP HER GET OVER HIM.

BRNNGG

Hey, Leo. You going to practice?

Yeah.

Not looking forward to the planks, though.

Ha, I hear you.

ADAM WELLER IS ON THE TRACK TEAM WITH ME. IT'S THE ONLY ACTIVITY I JOINED...

WHOOSH

... and I'm really good at

ADAM'S ALSO THE ONLY ONE WHO TALKS TO ME.

What's with Catalino? He never says anything.

He's too good for us. Just 'cause he's fast.

He's actually pretty nice.

Whatever.

HONESTLY, PART OF ME *WANTS* TO MAKE AN EFFORT. BUT PART OF ME...

Why don't you at least try to make friends?

What's the point? I'm not sticking around. I hate it there.

MY PLAN: TO WEAR MY PARENTS DOWN SO THEY'LL LET ME TRANSFER TO LAKEFRONT MIDDLE.

So far, there have been obstacles.

NOPE.

BUT I'M NOT GIVING UP!

ADAM AND I WALK TO THE LOCKER ROOM. GOTTA ADMIT, IT'S NICE TO HAVE COMPANY.

AS WE HEAD TO THE FIELD...

ok

ok what?

ok come 2 dance w me

sure?

sure 😊

↑
= Sarah in better mood

COOL! MY MOOD'S BETTER, TOO!

IT'LL BE FUN TO SEE MY OLD FRIENDS. I CAN'T WAIT TO SHOW 'EM:

my sick moves

78

AND MAYBE SOMEDAY, SOMEHOW...

... I'LL BE ABLE TO GO TO A SCHOOL WHERE I FIT IN.

SARAH

I asked him

Leo hasn't texted or stopped by in two days.

49½ hours,
not that I'm
counting

Okay, he responded after I texted him, but that doesn't count.

u mad?

u talking
2 me?

wanna come
ovr? my mom
made yoyos*
😊😊

*Mexican pastry
that looks like the
toy it's named for

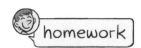

homework

This is the weirdest. First, because I can always lure Leo with sweets.

The Pied Piper

Second, because we've never been apart for more than a day, unless you count vacations. And for those, one of us usually tags along.

Towels. Check.

Sunscreen. Check.

BFF. Check.

That's BGF!

Then I notice the weirdest thing of all.

The heck?

They're in running clothes, so they all must be on the track team.

I should be glad, right? I mean, Leo's always resisted making friends at EW. Maybe he's finally broken down and gotten some.

I've been encouraging it. After all, his parents aren't gonna cave on private school. But he's stubborn. For a while, he let his grades drop, too (on purpose!). But that didn't help—in fact, his dads got nervous and just hired tutors around the clock . . . so Leo was cooped up all last fall, which drove him batty.

His grades finally improved, and he joined track. But that's where it ended. He still refused to make friends. And you've gotta understand . . . unlike me, Leo is pretty outgoing. I guess that's what drove me bonkers. Because where it takes extra effort for me to make and keep friends, this is something that comes natu-rally to Leo and he was **wasting** it.

It took me all of sixth grade and part of seventh to finally find school friends I'm comfortable with. It wasn't easy. Leo was only one of two friends I had in elementary school. Kerri

Kowalski was the other, and she pretty much abandoned me for the cool crowd in middle school.

I floated around for a while, mainly hanging out with some kids from art class and dance club, but I never really connected with anyone. Until Emmie. I was the one who reached out—not an easy move for me—and I'm **so** happy I did.

probably heading
to Taystee's

Maybe he still needs to cool off.

Maybe it's good for us to take a little break from each other.

Maybe it's also good he's making friends.

Then why am I feeling
miserable and confused?

I can't just sit here and be miserable, though. I get up and head outside myself.

Where are
you going,
Cachetona?

To Emmie's.
And stop
calling me
that!!

I hear her laugh. Grr.

I grab my bike and ride to Emmie's. She's not far. I usually text first, but this is just Plan A. Plan B is heading home and sketching more dress designs. An' if I'm not inspired, Plan C is helping my mom clean the dishes (normally Plan Z, but I'm pretty antsy).

Luckily, Emmie is home.

Inspiration strikes.

Poor Bri. Her bat mitzvah is less than a month away, and she's nervous.

I sit at Emmie's kitchen table while she finds us snacks.

Truth is, Mamá and I have gotten so used to being around sweets, we barely touch 'em anymore (except for those—mmm—donuts).

We talk and sketch and munch on orange and pear slices. It doesn't take long to forget about Leo.

We get back on track and come up with a few ideas for dance decor. Not too many in case it goes in a different direction, but enough to get people enthusiastic. So far, the theme is "Get Glowing" (glow-in-the-dark), which should be really fun.

I head back home before dinner, feeling twenty thousand times better. I even think of another dress design while riding. I wanna knock Ben's socks off.

regular, not burger-themed

About a block away from home, still lost in dress thoughts, I practically run over Leo and his two new friends.

Whoa!

Omigosh, I'm so sorry!

We stand there awkwardly for a moment.

Next-door neighbor??

They nod.

I don't know what to say after that.

I probably should've sounded more enthusiastic, but Leo's standing there, looking uncomfortable. Also, his house might as well be my own—I'm always running back and forth without permission—so it's weird to get an invite.

I go straight home and don't look back.

So, that's it, then?

I'm now just a **next-door neighbor?**

Fine. He can be that way. After all, I have other things I can do until he comes to his senses. Not just the decorating committee, but there's art club, poetry club, and now a dress to design and sew! I have a full, busy life, close friends, and a potential bf (please, please, please).

At least, that's what I tell myself.

Leo

She lost her nerve

IT'S SATURDAY. WE'RE WALKING TO TAYSTEE'S.

(a requirement since it's 90 degrees out)

I think I'll get a shake. They have Creamsicle this month.

I'm gonna get a slushie and pour it over my head.

Guess what? I designed a new dress for the dance!

Cool. Should I, like, match you or anything?

(giggle) No, silly, that's for high school proms. Wear jeans or whatever.

I'M ALMOST AS EXCITED FOR THE DANCE AS SHE IS. BUT FOR DIFFERENT REASONS.

I wanna see the inside of the school.

Will you tour me around?

Why? You're never gonna go there.

I'm wearing my parents down. You'll see.

SHE SHAKES HER HEAD. I KNOW SARAH'S SICK OF ME TALKING ABOUT THIS.

Whoa.

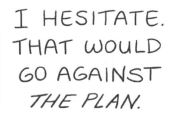

I HESITATE. THAT WOULD GO AGAINST *THE PLAN.*

Nah, thanks. We're just gonna get something to go.

See ya.

?

Why don't you want to sit with them? We don't have to leave.

I'd rather just walk. K?

Ohhkay.

MINT CHOCOLATE CHIP

ANANA SPLIT

WHILE IN LINE, I HEAR SOME-ONE CALLING.

voice that belongs to somebody three times his size

Lass!

Hi!

Where's your kilt? Afraid you'll get ice cream on it?

MENU

WE GET OUR SHAKES AND WAVE BYE TO EVERYONE.

Can you *please* stop complain-ing about your school? I'm really tired of it.

ffsssh

Okay.

Also...

...why *don't* you try harder to make friends? What's it gonna hurt? If you transfer, that doesn't mean you can't still hang out. Look at us.

Traitor.

STILL, SHE MAKES SENSE. AND SARAH ALWAYS LOOKS OUT FOR ME. SHE JUST WANTS ME TO BE... WELL, ME. AND "ME" IS:

friendly

likes people

hates being alone

loves burgers with <u>lots</u> of yellow mustard (just a factoid)

I'll try... maybe.

SHE LOOKS HAPPIER. WE KEEP WALKING AND SLURPING UNTIL WE GET HOME.

Gotta go. I'm having dinner at my uncle's tonight.

I WALK INSIDE AND TOSS MY CUP AWAY.

I HEAD RIGHT TO MALCOLM'S TANK. I POKE A PIECE OF LETTUCE AT HIM AND THINK.

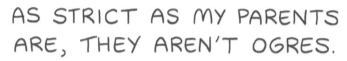

AS STRICT AS MY PARENTS ARE, THEY AREN'T OGRES.

I KNOW THEY'RE JUST LOOKING OUT FOR ME.

AND IT *PROBABLY* DIDN'T HELP THAT I GOOFED OFF IN ELEMENTARY SCHOOL.

I ALSO GET SARAH'S FRUSTRATION. I GRIPE NONSTOP ABOUT SCHOOL, AND EVERY- BODY HAS THEIR LIMIT.

poke

So I'll do what I promised and stop.

BUT AS FOR "MAKING AN EFFORT":

I'll try... maybe.

I'D BE LYING IF I SAID MY HEART WAS IN IT.

SARAH

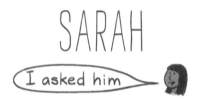

I asked him

As I said, it started about a year ago.

It was like one minute Ben was just some kid at school who happened to be:

← Leo's friend

The next:

← swoonworthy hotcake

sigh

I never developed a crush that fast. Okay, I'd never had a crush, period. I guess I just didn't know it could hit like a ton of . . . What's heavier than bricks?

made of cement

It's no fluke that it coincided with Ben's growth spurt and the fact that he finally grew into his ears and stopped tucking his shirt into his shorts. Not that looks matter that much to me (they don't), but it changed him in my eyes. He seemed older some-how, not the squeaky-voiced, silly, freckly little kid who played tackle-tag with Leo in the elementary school playground.

He got cooler, too. Or maybe quieter, hard to tell. I like that he's:

mysterious

thinking of cheese

Bri thinks that it's more important for a potential bf to be open, enthusiastic, and know how to make good conversation. But I prefer someone I can just be with.

Okay, I have no idea how I'd be with him, but at least I'll find out next Friday!

We've already started meeting for the decorations. There are about a dozen of us on the committee. Emmie and I presented the ideas we had come up with.

Okay, *I* presented them

eep

Everyone loved them! Ms. Laurie had us all brainstorm some more ideas. Then we divvied up what we're going to do. Emmie, Bri, and I will make cutout neon shapes to hang on the cafeteria walls. Everybody else will be in charge of:

black lights

glow-in-the-dark
face paint and accessories

selfie station

LAKEFRONT
GET GLOWING

neon ceiling
garlands

projectors for
glowy images

There's even enough in the budget for glow-in-the-dark punch
and snacks!

glow-in-the-
dark tummy

We got permission to skip classes and decorate the cafeteria on
the afternoon of the dance. Em is planning to come to my house
afterward to get ready. I asked Bri if she wanted to come, too, but
she's going to the dance straight from dinner at her aunt's.

(PS Emmie still hasn't asked Tyler.)

THWOMP

↖ kicking herself

All this would have me totally giddy except for a couple of things.

Thing 1   Thing 2

First, Leo is still avoiding me. It's now been a week, and he's barely acknowledged my existence. It's actually giving me bad flashbacks of sixth grade.

Seriously. Sarah *who?*

Every time I try to talk to him, he tells me he has too much homework ("private school load") or that he's tired from track. I'd **almost** buy it except I've seen him with his new friends—twice.

track field

I'm trying not to worry about it until after the dance, when I'll have more time to figure things out and he'll have had more time to cool off.

although, by now, you'd think he'd be downright chilly

Okay, I'm good.

And then there's Ben. Ever since I asked him to the dance, he hasn't exactly gone out of his way to ask me about plans. I've seen him in the halls, but either he hasn't seen me or he's been in a hurry. I did text to check if he wanted to be picked up for the dance or meet at school. He never responded. At first, it didn't bother me, 'cause even Leo gets frustrated about his text avoidance.

So I tried again two days later.

If only I could talk to Leo about it, he might have some advice. But how do I talk to my best friend about boy problems when my best friend . . .

* "my daughter"
(much better than Chubby-Cheeked)

I stop sewing.

Mamá, did you ever have boy problems?

She raises an eyebrow.

I mean, before Dad.

chuckle

Of course. Hard not to.

Started in eighth grade. I had a crush on a cute boy, but he liked my best friend.

She was the sweetest, though. She wouldn't pay him any attention out of loyalty to me.

Auntie Wendy?

That's Mama's best friend. She lives in another state, but they're still close. Mama nods.

I've had good experiences, too. Had a few serious boyfriends. Even your dad and I had some nice years before...

Her voice trails off.
We don't talk about him. Like, ever.
My parents divorced when I was two. They married and had me really young—my dad right out of college and Mama while she was still there (where they met). Mama said they were infatuated and rushed in against their parents' wishes.

invisible
cartoon
hearts

Money soon got really tight. My dad couldn't find a good job here, so he went to the West Coast to live with his parents, work, and save up. It was supposed to be temporary. But months turned into a year, and a year turned into:

meeting the "true"
love of his life

walking off into
the (California)
sunset

Her name is Sheila, but I call her "She-Devil" to Leo. Mama wouldn't like that. She says it's not her fault, and anyway, we've all moved on. I even took Mama's last name.

Dad now has a good job (he owns some sporting-goods stores) and sends us money, but practically the only time I ever hear from him is when I get a card on birthdays. And he always signs it, "—Brett."

<u>not</u>:

Love, Dad **OR** xo, Pops **OR EVEN** ☺ Brett

So I try to forget him.

Mama's had dates since my dad but nothing serious. She says she likes it being just the two of us. Her big dream is to go back to college (since she dropped out), get her business degree, and open an actual bakery.

Then I'll worry about a boyfriend... if I even want one.

She's already making her dream come true. Not just the catering business, but she's started taking classes. Only one per semester, since she works two jobs, but it's a start.

I'm so, so, so proud of her.

Right?

So what's the boy problem, mija?

It's Ben, the one I asked to the dance. Leo's friend.

I tell her about the texts.

Sweetie, you need to talk to him in person. Make him give you an answer.

I can't find him at school.

She frowns.

I'm not ready to talk about that, so I just ask:

She goes back in the kitchen to clean up for dinner, humming something I don't recognize.

probably from the dinosaur era (early 2000s)

I don't intend to call Ben (who **does** that?), but I have an idea. I race upstairs, taking my phone with me.

I plop on my beanbag. I'm determined to do this before I lose my nerve.

dialing number

hearing ringtone

=click=

Uh. Hello?

I hang up immediately.

I wait exactly thirty seconds.

One one-thousand...

And then . . .

srry. butt dialed u by mistke

Ben →

lol ok

btw......

IT ONLY TOOK ONE YEAR, NINE MONTHS, AND TWO WEEKS, BUT...

We know how unhappy you are at EW. But that unhappiness is much of your own making.

We'll consider— *consider* — sending you to Lakefront next school year.

MY JAW DROPS.

IF you make more of an effort *now*. Not just with grades, but making friends.

Adam Weller's mom said you were invited over after a meet, and you declined.

This is one of those examples of "making an effort," honey.

I WONDER IF I LOOK AS GUILTY AS I FEEL.

If, by fall, you're still seriously unhappy, then we'll see.

Think you can make that effort? And trust me, parents talk. We will *know.*

BACK IN MY ROOM, I FACETIME SARAH.

That's great! All you have to do is make friends. And you're good at that.

I don't *have* to. I just need to make an effort. That's all they said.

But...you told me you'd try.

I said *maybe.*

You're so infuriating. You know, I just want to see you happy again.

I will be. Once I'm at Lakefront.

SHE MAKES A FRUSTRATED NOISE.

You say that, but you've never gone there. How do you know it'll be any better?

Why aren't you on my side? Don't you want me there? You did all last year.

Of course! I just think...

SHE PAUSES.

I just think you're building it up in your head. And you never gave EW a chance.

And you promised your parents today. But you're not gonna do that. Not totally.

Also...

Yeah?

I do want you at my school. And yeah, I kept trying to convince you to go there all last year. But now I'm worried that if you come and it doesn't live up to your expectations...

...you'll blame me.

No way!

Just promise me you'll try.

I DON'T WANT TO.
IT'S ALMOST THE END OF THE
YEAR. WHAT'S THE POINT?

BUT I THINK OF MY PARENTS.

We just want you to thrive,
honey.

Like a
plant?

AND SARAH, WHO
JUST DOESN'T WANT
TO SEE ME LONELY
AT SCHOOL.

AND EVEN THOUGH I'M
FRUSTRATED, WHEN
ONLY FIVE MINUTES AGO
I WAS ELATED...

...THIS TIME I GIVE HER
MY WORD.

SARAH

I asked him

YES!!

 I whoop and kick up my legs, accidentally hurling my phone into my fake plant, Fiona.

gulp

buuurp

 It worked! I got Ben to answer my text. And now we have **definite** plans for the dance.

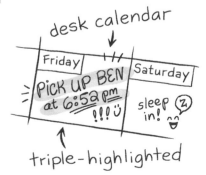

desk calendar

Friday

Saturday

PICK UP BEN at 6:52 pm !!! ☺

sleep in! 💤

triple-highlighted

I barely see Ben the following week. But that's okay. I look forward to our magical night together. I don't even worry so much about Leo. I still figure he'll come around, and I promise myself that I'll talk to him right after the dance.

In the meantime, I do the usual stuff: go to school, hang out with Emmie and Bri, do homework, and go to art and poetry clubs. I'm **really** enjoying poetry club. I've sort of made some new friends there, too.

Ruby

Leah

Juan

Juan's funny drawing

Which makes me wonder if Leo is still friendly with those kids from his track team.

It makes me feel weird. Like, almost . . . jealous? I don't know why, 'cause we both have other friends and still manage to be BFFs.

Or **did**.

Maybe that's why I feel weird. Maybe it's 'cause our friendship is on shakier ground and I'm worried.

friendship earthquake

rumble

I remind myself—again—that I'll talk to him after the dance.

Besides, I'm super busy with all that stuff I mentioned, plus I'm working on the decorating committee and putting the final touches on my dress.

It looks so good. Mamá and I decided to model it after a Chiapas dress (traditional costume from Mexico):

off-the-shoulder

flower embroidery (used pre-made ones)

flowy skirt

← favorite color combo: charcoal and pink

It's funny: even though I'm kinda quiet and don't really try to stand out, I love experimenting with fashion. I know I get weird looks sometimes, but that's how it goes when you wanna be "cutting edge" (Mamá's words).

In a strange way, it also helps me weed out the people I don't want to be around. If someone doesn't like what I'm wearing, then I don't bother with them. So, I think it's good that Kerri Kowalski ditched me (I can say now), 'cause she started giving me looks and whispering to her friends all the time. She didn't think I knew, but I did.

Anyway, my real friends always compliment my creations.

Including Leo. But then, he likes wearing fun things, too. That's another reason he complains about EW—he has to wear a uniform all the time. At least he's allowed to show his personality with:

novelty socks!

eye-balls

bacon

burgers

ugly feet

Malcolm,
Leo's bearded
dragon
(custom-made)

I've really gotta take my mind off him.

I already finished homework, and I'm getting kinda antsy. Mamá used to say I have ants in my pants if I don't have something to do all the time.

I text Emmie.

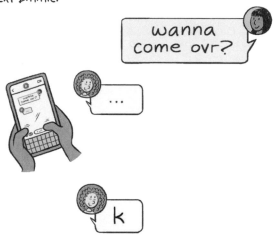

wanna
come ovr?

...

k

Huh. She seems down—or as down as I'm able to read in a text.

She rings the doorbell about ten minutes later.

We go up to my room and enter the crawl space. I close the door for privacy and turn on the fairy lights. It's a little hot in here (hot in the warm months, chilly in the winter), so I peel off my hoodie.

Yeah. I even made a cute drawing.

Emmie's sketchbook

← drawing of Van Gogh's *Starry Night*

↳ swirlies ↗

I had my sketchbook with me. I was gonna show it to him in the art room after school, 'cause we both wanted to work on our ceramics project.

Ms. Laurie is having us make all these crazy pinch pots. Mine are funny animals with giant square teeth.

↑ dog

mystery rodent

I didn't stick around. I felt sick and I didn't want them to see me. I went home.

I still feel kinda sick.

Celia has that effect on people.

Emmie breaks into a little smile. But it's gone in an instant.

So, is he going with her?

I guess. This means they'll probably start dating again.

I missed my chance. Not that I ever really had one....

Of course you did. I've seen the way Tyler looks at you.

What do you mean?

Ever since the Student Showcase, I've seen him look at you. Like, different.

That's what Bri says. But I've never noticed.

Of course not. He does it when you're not looking, silly.

Anyway, he'll come around. When he and Celia were a couple, he got so annoyed.

Maybe he just has amnesia.

Emmie laughs, and I know she feels better. We head downstairs, where I convince Mamá (pretty easily) to give Emmie a vanilla concha from the batch she's baking for a quinceañera.

eyes lighting up

Mamá laughs.

That solves most of the world's problems, doesn't it?

OMG

Chef's Kiss

Afterward, we ride our bikes to Brianna's mom's condo, where a frustrated Bri waits.

We ride our bikes to Taystee's.

When we get there, there's a small line. But this time, no one we know is waiting in it.

If he likes me, why wouldn't he ask *me*?

Maybe 'cause Conniving Cee got to him first.

I just think he's kinda shy that way. He seems confident all the time 'cause he's popular, but when it comes to crushes...

...everyone's pretty insecure.

I think of Ben. Maybe he is, too.

So maybe I do have a chance . . . ?

After we finish our cones, we head home in different directions.

Sometimes I forget how high our driveway apron is. Popping my bike tire onto it, I nearly flip over when I see Leo coming out of his back gate.

Instead, I manage to stumble off my bike (not very gracefully) just as it drops sideways.

undies

OMG.
Leo rushes over as I manage to get to my feet.

We look at each other awkwardly. I try to give him a harsh look, but . . .

sneaking back into yard

Leo gives me a funny look. He's no longer smiling or laughing.

He turns around.

I wave a half-hearted bye and head up the porch steps. Walking into the house, I accidentally slam the screen door.

I'm not even mad that she called me 'Cachetona,' I'm too . . . what's the word?

Distraught.

↰ Winn Word

I head upstairs. Mamá's making my favorite dinner, pollo asado. But even the amazing smell doesn't affect me.

Leo keeps avoiding me. I break my promise to myself and start worrying again.

It's the first time in a long time . . .

. . . I'm not thinking about Ben.

HE PAUSES THE GAME AND
THROWS ME EXTRA SWIM
SHORTS FROM A DRAWER.
I CHANGE IN THE BATHROOM.

OKAY, MUCH BETTER.

I GROAN. MY *TWO* BEST FRIENDS. THIS ISN'T HAPPENING.

Actually... I was *afraid* this would happen.

Sarah's really nice, not weird. She just tries to please people.

Well, she tries way too hard with me, and it's creepy.

I don't care if you're friends with her. Just keep her away from me.

Whaddya think I've been doing?

SARAH

Friday. Morning of the dance.
And I don't see Ben anywhere.

He's usually one of the first ones here, like me. Not 'cause he loves school that much, but 'cause his dad drops him off on the way to work. Leo told me Ben would rather get a ride and come early than sit on the funky-smelling bus.

I'm early just 'cause my bus has the closest route. I usually see Ben at his locker around this time. Except when he's sick.

uh-oh.

I wait a few extra minutes just in case. No sign of him. Soon the hallway gets crowded as more kids get dropped off.

shuffle

Joe jigs over. I'm so distracted, I barely register that he's right in front of me. When I do, I try to smile.

I keep looking down the hallway.

I quickly close my locker door and race down the hallway, dodging people, backpacks, and angry hall monitors.

I try not to panic. I keep Emmie company at her locker while she puts away her stuff. Bri soon arrives.

It's a Hebrew prayer. I finally had a breakthrough.

That's great, Bri!

You guys will be impressed. That's *if* I don't have a panic attack and throw up on the altar flowers.

They laugh, but I'm still peering down the hall.

What's with her?

Ben hasn't shown up.

Oh, he's probably just running late or something.

Besides, it's Friday. Half the kids are tardy when it's nice on a Friday.

It **is** nice. Sunny and warm. All good signs for a great evening. No dark and threatening clouds to foreshadow bad events.

Like being ditched.

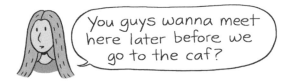

You guys wanna meet here later before we go to the caf?

Decorating. Instead of afternoon classes.

(sigh) Sure. Just wish I was looking forward to the dance. I don't wanna watch Tyler and Celia's PDA...

...where we eat our tater tots.

Even though I'm anxious, I try to cheer her up.

It'll still be fun.

That's right. We don't need *men* to enjoy the dance.

We have each other. And music. And lots and lots of neon llamas.

neon cut-outs
for the dance:

Lakefront
mascot

Emmie and I smile. If anything, decorating will be fun.
The bell rings, and we head to our homerooms.

BRNNG

I don't see Ben the rest of the morning. But I try not to
worry—after all, I don't always see him around. We're on separate school teams. (Lakefront is so big, the classes are divided into
groups or "teams" with their own teachers.)

team names:

The Petri Dishes

Punctuation Patrol

Let's eat kids!

Later, I meet Emmie and Bri at Em's locker, like we agreed. We walk to the caf together, joking around. I'm trying to stay cheerful even though a big part of me is worried.

We decorate all afternoon. When we're done, the place looks unrecognizable. Our neon cutouts—glued to black tablecloths—cover the walls, windows, and even the tray counter. Colorful neon garlands and LED balloons dangle from the ceiling. Tin trays—filled with giveaway glow necklaces and wristbands—decorate tabletops where glow-in-the-dark punch and candy (regular but with neon wrappers) will be passed out. We also made a doodle wall that people can decorate using thick neon pens.

And that's not all. We also thought of games: Ping-pong ball toss (into glow-in-the-dark cups) and a ring toss using glow bracelets and old bottles filled with sand and decorated with neon stickers.

180

By the time we're finished, we barely make it to the bus.

Emmie's coming home with me so we can get ready for the dance together. We sit down, catching our breath, and check our phones. Emmie checks for texts from her mom while I check for . . .

hey cant make it 2nite. sick. rly srry

My phone drops into my lap. I think I'm sick, too.

Ohh, Sarah, that stinks.

Yeah.

But hey! It'll still be fun, okay? We'll take lots of pictures of our decorations and tons of selfies, and we'll *dance* so much!

Yeah. Sure.

But I don't mean it. How can I have a good time now? I don't even know if he skipped school on purpose to avoid going with me or if he's really, truly sick.

The avoiding part wouldn't even be the worst. It's the "not knowing" part.

My eyes fill with tears.

Reminds me so much of my dad. I'm never sure if he wants a relationship with me. There's always a little part of me that holds on to hope that he does. And I'm always left wondering.

Boys.

Yeah, I know. But there's Leo. He's great!

Not really.

I explain what's been going on.

I didn't really say anything 'cause... well, I thought it'd pass.

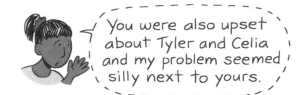

You were also upset about Tyler and Celia and my problem seemed silly next to yours.

It's not silly.
He's your "BBF."
That's huge.
Huger, actually.

She hugs me, which helps. A little.
We get off the bus and walk to my house.

Oh no!
I think I
dropped my
favorite
scrunchie.

Go ahead, I'll
be right back!

I don't say anything. I really don't feel like helping her look.
I just wanna go inside and lie down.
And I **definitely** don't wanna go to the dance.

I plop on the couch and stare at the ceiling, smelling the irre-
sistible scent of cooling donuts.

At least I have Emmie and Bri, I tell myself. . . .

. . . and my wonderful, wonderful mamá.

Leo She lost her nerve

THE GOOD NEWS: BEN PROMISED NOT TO TELL ANYONE SARAH'S SECRET.

Oh, no way I will.

THE BAD NEWS: OUR CONVO AFTERWARD.

Say what?

I said I'm not coming over anymore. Like ever.

She's always... lurking.

It's not "lurking" when she's invited.

You know what I mean. An' now it's doubly creepy.

She *likes* you; she's not gonna *butcher* you.

Have you ever *watched* a horror movie?

HE KNOWS I HAVEN'T, EXCEPT ONCE.

Flashback:

AHHHHHH!

baby-sitter →

horror film

Look, it's no big deal. You can just keep coming to my house.

I guess. But, dude, I've gotta be honest...

What?

I STOP MYSELF.

Your house is boring as all— *mmph!*

YEAH, I PROMISED TO TRY TO MAKE NEW FRIENDS, BUT I'M NOT READY TO LOSE THE ONES I HAVE.

Even if the only thing on his mind is shooting zombies.

Let's not forget cheese.

I'M IN MY ROOM NOW, PLAYING TUG-OF-WAR WITH MALCOLM AND HALF A GRAPE.

distracted

winning

IT'S THE DAY BEFORE THE DANCE. ON ONE HAND, I'M LOOKING FORWARD TO IT.

wearing real clothes

dancing

checking out the school

squint

ON THE OTHER, IT JUST REMINDS ME OF SARAH AND HOW I'LL HAVE TO KEEP HER AWAY FROM BEN.

HEEEY, is that the principal doing karaoke?

whip

slorp

I WISH SHE HAD NEVER TOLD ME HER SECRET...

:plink:

secret crush

SARAH

I wish I'd never asked Ben to the dance!

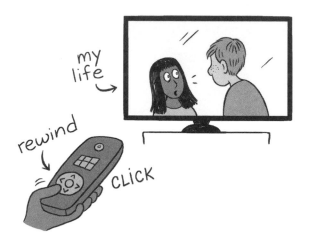

I'm still on the couch. Mamá consoled me and then went back to baking, promising to save Emmie and me the largest donuts of the batch.

But I really can't eat.

would rather count dents in the floor *

* "character," as Mama calls it

...twenty... twenty-one...

sewing machine mishap
(aka the-incident-that-shall-
not-be-named)

Soon, Emmie walks in.

Did you find your scrunchie?

I didn't really drop it.

Then why—?

Mamá must have some mystical power over us; I wasn't hungry, but suddenly I can hear all three of our stomachs growl at once.

hunger harmony

She smiles and heads back to the kitchen.
I stare at Leo, not knowing what to do or say.

Hey.

Hi.

Emmie told me what happened.

Oh God. You don't need to feel sorry for me or anything.

No, it's not that. An' I don't know if Ben is really sick. That's not why I'm here.

I'm just... apologizing.

You know. For acting all... weird and distant and stuff.

I shouldn't have blown you off like that.

I get it, Leo. I was acting like a dork in front of Ben, which embarrassed you.

Also, I shouldn't have asked him to the dance. It put you in a weird spot.

So I'm sorry, too.

No, it's...

Well, okay, that was part of the reason I got upset.

That hits me in the gut.

He guessed. I'm so embarrassed. But also relieved that it's out in the open. Still . . .

Something doesn't feel right. To completely **avoid** your best friend and not talk about the whole situation? That's not like Leo.

Then again, everyone seems to be changing all the time. Mamá says that's how it is for middle schoolers. One minute, you're a kid. The next, you're growing up and making questionable choices based on pure **feelings.**

I nod. He grins and leans down to give me a big hug. It's like a warm blanket. Even though I'm still upset about Ben, it feels so good to have Leo back.

Even Emmie's changing.

braver

also 1 ½ inches taller since winter

(too-short pants)

She and Leo glance at each other.

Are you still going to the dance?

I don't think so.

Sarah, you made a beautiful dress. An' helped decorate. You should definitely go.

Also, if you want...

I laugh. I can't help it.

204

I look at my two friends, who've never seemed so eager for an answer.

I'm still not sure it's a good idea, and I'm still upset, but I don't want to let them down. Also . . . I realize I don't want Ben to get the best of me. Whether he ditched me on purpose or not.

Okay.

They cheer, and I'm suddenly squashed in a hug.

warm, toasty
sandwich

As if on cue, Mamá comes out of the kitchen with a pile of gigantic fresh donuts sprinkled with sugar crystals. Not sure if she overheard anything, but I don't really mind. Unlike a lot of other kids and their parents, I don't hide much from her.

Like Emmie's, Leo's parents are health conscious. But they're not as strict about it.

We take the donuts outside so we don't get crumbs on the floor. After we eat, Emmie goes back inside to use the bathroom. Leo stands up and dusts sugar off his pants.

He starts running toward his house.
But stops.

I start tearing up again a little. I can't help it.

Leo

She lost her nerve

Thanks! See ya later.

Hi, kiddo.

Well?

SLAM

We wouldn't dream of it.

WHAT DO THEY CALL IT IN BOOKS WHEN SOMETHING CHANGES AND TOTALLY AFFECTS THE PLOT?

YEAH. I FEEL LIKE THAT'S WHERE I'M AT.

ADAM INVITED LANEY AND ME TO HIS HOUSE AFTER SCHOOL.

THIS TIME I WENT.

I HAD STARTED THINKING ABOUT SARAH AND MY PROMISE TO MAKE FRIENDS.

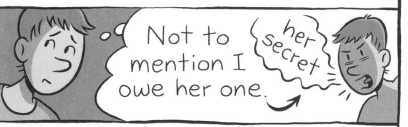

Not to mention I owe her one.

her secret

ALSO, I WANTED TO SHOW MY PARENTS THAT I WAS TRYING.

I DIDN'T EVEN HAVE TO TRY THAT HARD. WE CLICKED WITHOUT MUCH EFFORT. AND THEN:

track teammates

I HATE TO ADMIT IT, BUT I HAD MORE FUN WITH THEM THAN I HAD WITH BEN ALL YEAR.

BESIDES, IT *IS* NICE HAVING PEOPLE TO HANG WITH.

...JUST UNTIL I CHANGE SCHOOLS.

SO IF YOU WERE WONDERING...

WHOOOSH

shrug

Plunk

...*YES*, I STILL WANT TO GO TO LAKEFRONT.

OKAY, EW'S NOT *THAT* BAD.
I'VE GOT SOME GOOD TEACHERS.
AND A NICE COACH.
BUT THAT'S WHERE IT ENDS.

I *SAID*, THAT'S
WHERE IT ENDS!

BESIDES, I DON'T HAVE TIME FOR THIS...

...I'VE GOTTA GET READY FOR A DANCE.

SARAH

218

I had painted each of my fingernails a different color. And then I painted Emmie's like mine. In solidarity, Bri did hers the same way.

Leo didn't follow my advice to wear regular clothes. But that's okay. He's a lot like me when it comes to fashion. Outside of school dress codes, he doesn't follow any rules. Especially when it comes to matching.

Hawaiian shirt

odd-colored shorts

his Malcolm socks

I was worried he might be a little extra for Em and Bri, but they really get a kick out of him. Besides, he's so friendly and fun, it's hard not to love him.

wave of affection

I promise myself I'll never keep secrets from him again.

FOOMP

And he'd better not, either!

I have to admit, even without Ben, I'm having so much fun! It was definitely a good idea to bring Leo. Before we went to the caf, I showed him around. At first, he was excited to see it all, but in the end, I don't think he was that impressed. I mean, he goes to an expensive private school—I'm sure everything is fancier there.

He was definitely happy to see some old friends. Although . . .
I noticed once he said hi and they talked . . .

Only a minute later:

Luckily, we got him dancing, and he was in his element. No Pigeon Waddle, but he still had some (ahem) unique moves.

Eggbeater

Jazz Rabbit

Duck Hustle

Tyler is having "glow" punch with Anthony and Joe on one side of the cafeteria. Joe is also tossing candy in the air and trying to catch it in his mouth.

She points to the entrance, where Celia and her friends are checking out the decorations. Celia isn't looking very impressed.

too cool for everything

LET'S GLOW

Wow.

We both look at Emmie.

That seems to spark something in Emmie. She kinda straightens up, glances over at Tyler, looks back at us, and . . .

I'll be back.

Where's she going?

Omigod. No way!

Dev

Leo and I look at each other.

He hints at doing the Pigeon Waddle till I play-punch him.

I head toward the cafeteria doorway when I hear something that stops me.

...Friedman really sick? 'Cause he was fine at practice yesterday.

EXIT

Ben's softball teammates

Nah. I texted him. He stood up that girl in the weird dress. Didn't want anyone thinking she was his gf.

That's cold.

He only said yes 'cause she took him by surprise.

An' I guess he didn't wanna hurt her feelings. They have the same friend— that kid from EW.

They leave. But I can't seem to move.
So Ben really did blow me off.
It wasn't just a bad feeling.

finally
found
my legs

I was wrong.

The "not knowing" isn't the worst part.

Leo

She lost her nerve

THE DANCE.

I MAY BE GETTING CARRIED AWAY (JUST A LITTLE). BUT I CAN'T HELP THAT I HAVE RHYTHM.

LEO'S GUIDE TO SMOOTH MOVES:

1. Circle your friends while doing the "slide-glide"*:

 *invented and trade-marked

2. Spin around several times (just until you see stars).

3. Show off signature moves (aka squiggles, squirms, worms, kicks*)

shaka *avoid teachers

4. Repeat.
5. Repeat.
6. Repeat until someone (aka Sarah) says:

STOP! but I live 4 disco

looking for Ben

He's not here.

Did he text you?

Yeah, said he wasn't sure if he's coming.

THAT'S NOT QUITE TRUE. I LEFT OUT AN IMPORTANT PART.

wanna go but idk

if RWR is there, mab not good idea

stop calling her that

SARAH LOOKS DISAPPOINTED. BUT I'M HOPING BEN WON'T SHOW. IT'D JUST BE EASIER.

twirling: tried and true deflection technique

EARLY ON, SARAH SHOWED ME AROUND.

TRUTH IS, EW IS NICER. LIKE, A *LOT* NICER. BUT I EXPECTED THAT.

I STILL WANNA GO HERE, SO I MEMORIZED EVERY-THING. I MEAN *EVERYTHING.*

media center

recycling bins

water fountains

misfiring

bath-rooms

dead rat*

*Lakefront fixture since 2003

Make way! Neon oatmeal cookie!

ZIP

SARAH STILL THINKS I'M NUTS, BUT MY MIND'S MADE UP. EVEN IF THINGS *HAVE* BEEN BETTER AT EW.

Laney

hanging out tommw nt. my house. u in?

=blip=

BUT THAT'S TOTALLY SEPARATE.

THAT DUDE FROM TAYSTEE'S.
WITH THE JOKES.

FOR SOME REASON, I DON'T MENTION HIM TO SARAH.

Thanks.

After this, you wanna go play some games or—

He's here!

I TURN AND SEE BEN WALK IN WITH SOME FRIENDS FROM SOFTBALL.

groaaan

SHE HEADS TO THE REST-ROOM. MAYBE SHE'LL CHICKEN OUT WITH BEN.

I hope so.

ZIP

Hey, guys.

Hey. Where's your friend?

Bathroom.

I didn't think you'd be here.

No choice. Dean's sister is on the decorating committee and was rounding up people.

She can be bossy.

Is what's-her-name still crushing on me?

If so, lemme know when she's coming. I'll hide in the bathroom, too.

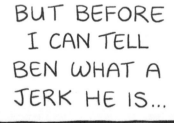

BUT BEFORE I CAN TELL BEN WHAT A JERK HE IS...

HA ha ha HA

SHE RUNS BACK TO THE
RESTROOM.

Sarah!

SHE POKES HER HEAD OUT. FOR A SECOND I'M RELIEVED. MAYBE SHE'LL LISTEN TO ME.

Just go hang out with those jerks. Get a ride with them.

AND LEAVE ME ALONE!

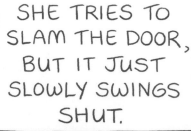

SHE TRIES TO SLAM THE DOOR, BUT IT JUST SLOWLY SWINGS SHUT.

(poor → dramatic effect)

OH MAN. I DID IT. I REALLY DID IT.

Incoming!!

errant neon slime

WZZZZ

Sorry!

YEP. I MADE A MESS OF EVERYTHING.

SARAH

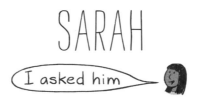

I asked him

For a while, I don't come out of the bathroom.

I wonder how many people do this . . . sit in a stall crying.
It's middle school, so I'm guessing a lot.

IT'S BEEN
0 DAYS
SINCE SOMEONE
HAS CRIED
IN THIS STALL.

I feel so humiliated. I should've known. My gut told me Ben didn't wanna go to the dance with me. I should've listened.

Girls keep coming and going. I try to stay quiet. At one point, I hear a lone girl walk in, but I can't tell who it is. She's in the stall next to me for a long time. When she's done, I hear her washing up at the sink.

Is that—?

Ruby Donovan. She's in some of my classes and we both belong to poetry club. Well, she goes more than me. She's really passionate about it.

She's also a lot better at writing than speaking. But that's okay.

I flush the toilet and come out. I'm sure my eyes are all puffy. Between that and my usual chubby cheeks, my face probably looks like a big marshmallow.

I burst into tears.

I laugh. I can't help it.

We stand there awkwardly for a second while I wipe my eyes a little too forcefully.

Ruby pauses, then takes my arm kinda gruffly and leads me to the sink. She grabs a paper towel and runs it under some water.

I take the damp towel and pat my sore eyes. She waits with me until they start looking a little better. Definitely less marshmallow-y.

If you want, I can start a rumor about him. I only have, like, five followers on SnapGab, but they're pretty fierce.

giggle

That's okay.

We walk out together. I'm feeling a little more human. Ruby heads back to the caf.

You okay?? I was waiting for you, and you were taking forever.

Yeah. No. Um, can we go over there?

I point to a back stairwell. We head over and sit down. I tell him what happened.

He doesn't say anything for a while.

It isn't lost on me that I totally put Leo in the middle. Normally, he'd take my side in an instant. But this is his good friend who blew me off, not some random seventh-grade dirtbag.

It's my fault. I shouldn't have asked him.

That seems to jerk him back into reality.

Forget him, BGF. Let's go dance.

But I—

C'mon. I'm gonna make you forget all about... who's-his-face!

He grins.

And I can't help it. I grin back. Not that I'm feeling anywhere near good, but Leo has a way of getting me out of my head.

We walk back to the cafeteria, and Leo pulls me onto the dance floor right away. I already feel a little better. Emmie, Tyler, Bri, and Dev join us. I notice Celia, dancing nearby, glaring at Emmie.

You're ticking off Miss Popularity, Emmie Douglass.

She had asked Tyler to the dance and didn't notice he never said yes.

She took him by surprise.

I swallow. "Took him by surprise." Sounds familiar.

Leo must've seen my face fall, because he grabs my hands and swings me around again. I squeal, laughing.

After the song ends and Leo goes to get some water . . .

He kinda stammers, and at first I'm not sure what he's trying to say.

I laugh and we head to the dance floor.

As much fun as I'm trying to have, it still feels like there's a big hole in my heart.

But I try to stay upbeat. I mean, that's what I do, right? I'm Sarah Reyes, nicest girl at Lakefront Middle School. Whatever happens, I smile through it.

crackle crrrack

Even if it's getting harder and harder.

Leo

ON A "FEELING LIKE A PILE OF GARBAGE" SCALE OF 1-10...

RIDING HOME WITH BEN. HIS SISTER, SOPHIA, IS DRIVING.

WHEN SOPHIA GOT HER LICENSE, SHE WAS SO EXCITED. BUT HER PARENTS PUT A DAMPER ON THAT QUICKLY.

STILL, IT MUST BE NICE TO HAVE A LICENSE. AND A CAR.

Then I wouldn't be here.

HERE BEING: NEXT TO SOMEONE I'M NOT EAGER TO BE AROUND.

So Sarah got sick and left?

Yeah.

bopping to Bluetooth/ tuned us out

WHEN I ASKED HIM FOR A RIDE HOME, I DIDN'T SAY A WORD ABOUT HER OVER-HEARING US. THAT'D MAKE EVERYTHING EVEN WORSE.

Dude, drop it, okay?

It's not like she's your girlfriend. Stop acting like she is.

Dude!

Keep it down, peons. Cabin Fever is on.

fave band

SOON, SHE PULLS IN TO MY DRIVEWAY.

Thanks, Sophia. Later, Ben.

If you change your mind, I'm doing a multiplayer roundup tomorrow. Us versus the bots!

I DON'T RESPOND. I JUST HEAD IN, CLOSE THE DOOR, AND GO UPSTAIRS.

(parents on a rare date night)

I ASK MYSELF — FOR THE HUNDREDTH TIME LATELY — WHY I'M STILL FRIENDS WITH BEN.

It's not like we have much in common anymore.

SARAH

This was NOT the night I had planned.

I'm still so hung up about Ben. The only reason the dance wasn't a total disaster was 'cause Leo was there.

But something keeps nagging at me: the fact that Leo went from being my best friend to avoiding me to being my best friend again. It makes me feel . . . well . . .

fwwPP

head
literally
spinning

I don't think he was telling the truth. That he was upset 'cause I kept my crush on Ben a secret. At least, I don't think it's the whole truth. I mean, I know him. He's **not** an avoider. Leo likes to talk things out.

yap yap
yap yak
yap

...and talk,
and talk,
and talk..

Maybe I just thought I knew him.

And even though I don't know Ben well—obvies—I thought he was a nice boy, at least.

Apparently, I know nothing about the male species.

Male Species [noun]: *syn*: dude, bro, brah. Often elusive; good at reducing girls to ugly-tears.

No. Sarah, you can't. Don't even think it.

But, I tell myself, I need to talk things over with someone objective. Someone male. With experience.

BAD, BAD idea.

I can't.

I've tried too many times in the past.

But this is what happens: either my dad's busy at one of his stores, distracted by Sheila and her three labradoodles, or just doesn't know what to say (pretty much like me, that last part).

Also, there's that other thing:

There's just no guy I can go to about all this.

Once in a while, I talk to Leo's parents if Mamá's busy or I need extra advice. But this is just too private.

I admit, sometimes I get jealous of Leo's relationship with his dads 'cause they're so hands-on. Yes, I have Mamá and she's great, but she gets busy. And tired. And I don't want to always bother her. At least with Leo, if one parent isn't around, the other usually is. And although he says they can be . . .

. . . they are a loving team. Something my mom and dad definitely are *not*.

You'd think I'd cry. The fact that I can't (or won't) call my own dad. But I'm so numb, I'm almost—literally—petrified. So I just sit still. Really, really still.

like → this

← petrified tree

Maybe that's good.

'Cause it's the only thing that can keep me from feeling anything.

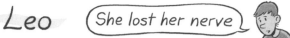
Leo · She lost her nerve

IT'S SATURDAY. I'VE TEXTED SARAH SO MUCH, I'M SURPRISED MY THUMBS HAVEN'T FALLEN OFF.

THIS IS REALLY UNLIKE HER. SHE MUST BE A WHOLE OTHER LEVEL OF UPSET.

I REALIZE I HAVE TO DO SOMETHING DRASTIC OR I'LL LOSE MY BEST FRIEND.

"Keep my BGF" hacks:

Post tear-jerking, glowing stuff about her on SnapGab

forgot why she was mad

Bribe her with milkshakes for life

yum!! TAYS-TEE'S

shake times a million

Offer to clean her porch (yuck)

scratch scratch

big idea

TWO HOURS LATER, I'M KNOCKING ON SARAH'S DOOR.

Leo! Hi, honey. Sarah's not here.

Oh.

She's out with her grandma and aunt.

Do you want to come in? That's a lot to balance.

Nah, that's okay. I'll come back.

She should be home anytime now.

Um, would it be okay if I wait on the porch?

Sure, it's your spot, hon. You want any-thing to eat or...?

That's okay. Thanks, Ms. R.

SHE GOES INSIDE. IN THE MEANTIME, I SPREAD THE CONTENTS OF MY BOXES ON THE PORCH.

AFTERWARD, I TAKE ROOT ON SARAH'S STEPS.

AND WAIT.

SARAH

I asked him

Mamá finds me.

I was calling you earlier and you didn't answer. I thought you had gone to sleep.

I say nothing.
Mamá sits next to me on the floor.

I find my voice. Barely.

Mamá sighs like it's her last breath.

Then she reaches over and hugs me.

I can't even cry. It's like I wasted all my tears on a boy who couldn't care less about me . . . and now I have no tears left for my own dad.

Her words trail off.

We're so quiet, I start to notice other sounds.

laptop
humming

clock
ticking

highway
buzzing

heart
breaking

Mija, I don't have all the answers.

But I do know one thing.

I look at her.

We can't help what others do. The only thing we can do is be the best people we can be, right?

I nod a little.

And to love ourselves. It's not always easy, but it's necessary.

And a part of that means surrounding ourselves with people who choose to love us back. That's something you're already doing, honey.

Sniffling, I think of Tía Elena and my grandma—people not of my choosing but who I'm lucky to have in my life.

I think about Emmie and Brianna. Friends I chose who chose me back.

And I think about Leo.

Mamá's right. I can't help it if some people aren't willing to share their lives with me. But I have plenty who do.

I think I know what to do now.

Mamá chuckles and squeezes me as we head downstairs.

Leo

She lost her nerve

I SIT AND WAIT FOR ABOUT HALF AN HOUR.

What's all this?

photo collage Sarah and I created in fourth grade

badly sewn shirt Sarah made me last year

jars of pennies we started collecting in first grade

stickers

one for Malcolm

lampshade we decoupaged with favorite comics

hamburger stress ball she got for my 12th b-day

short stories we wrote together about made-up superheroes

other "Sarah" gifts: favorite basketball, cornhole beanbags, fancy flashlight

Leo!

glop

Why — What is this?

Sar, we've been best friends forever, right?

Yeah, but *you*—

Hear me out.

SHE STAYS QUIET. SHE HAS A LOOK ON HER FACE THAT I'VE NEVER SEEN.

confused-but-determined-to-torture-me look

I just wanted to show you our history.

I made one mistake. A bad one, yeah.

But compare that to all *this*.

SHE LOOKS. AND SIGHS.

Aha! A smile!

Leo...

Look, can we just talk?

AS AN ANSWER, SHE SITS ON THE STOOP. I JOIN HER.

I'm really sorry, Sar. Ben was a total jerk. And so was I, for letting it slip that you like him.

SHE DOESN'T SPEAK FOR A MOMENT.

Correction.

Huh?

Liked.

Oh.

SHE BUMPS ME WITH HER SHOULDER AND I BUMP BACK.

I forgive you. Anyway, I thought about it. It's better that I know the truth.

Oh. That's good. 'Cause I made that cake so we could celebrate being friends again.

Or to say I'm sorry. Whichever.

SHE GIGGLES, AND WE GO SIT AT THE TABLE.

Even though I was happy to take you to the dance, I think I was using you a little.

Oh. You mean to get to Ben?

I'm sorry.

Hey, we're even. Well, not really. What I did was worse.

Leo...?

Were you embarrassed to have Ben over 'cause of the goofy way I acted around him?

Be honest.

Partly.

But also...

twirl

OMG. AM I REALLY ABOUT TO SAY IT?

It's mainly 'cause...

...I wished it was me you acted goofy around.

SARAH

I asked him

For once, we're sitting on his stoop and talking.

(hey, change can be good)

I told him about the (failed) call to my dad. And how bad I'm really feeling about everything.

That's a lot, Sar.

Yeah.

Well, I'm glad you're talking to me. Getting it off your chest and all that.

Um. Well. That's the other thing that's been bothering me.

You.

"who, me?" look

Leo... I need to know.

Why'd you stay away before the dance? Those were some of the worst weeks of my life.

Even worse than the Ben thing.

He doesn't respond. I try not to say anything, because it looks like he's gathering his thoughts.

Truth is I got upset...
not just 'cause you kept
your crush on Ben from me,
or 'cause you asked him
to the dance, but because...

He exhales.

You asked
the *wrong* guy
to the dance.

What do
you mean?

He just looks at me and raises his eyebrows.

"like,
hello?"

Which doesn't register at first.
Then . . .

Is...is that why you started hanging out with those new friends from school?

Yeah, partly. Also, 'cause you wanted me to.

I feel a huge urge to run inside my house. But I don't.

Leo...

Yeah, I know.

Look, I'll go now. This is... a lot, I guess.

Anyway, it's late. One of my dads will be hollering out the window any second.

He gets up and heads inside.
Neither of us says bye. Or does our usual BBF/BGF thing.
Instead, I go home.

(finally) remembering not to slam screen door

Despite everything that's happened tonight, I fall asleep super quickly. Feels like all my feelings formed a giant brick in my head and knocked me out.

I spend the weekend avoiding Leo. Luckily it pours, which helps. I try not to think about our habit of watching lightning shows from my porch. Instead, I stay inside and help my mom bake, do my homework, read, and sew while watching TV.

hemming shorts so they'll stop getting caught on bike seat

The next week, I go to school and actively hide from Ben.

I also keep my distance from Leo.

He hasn't texted me. I guess he's trying to give me space. It's not like I don't miss him, but how can I face him? Leo's like my brother. I've never seen him any other way.

"brother" lens

His new friends come over after practice a few times, although I haven't noticed Ben coming around. From my window, I see them eating snacks in his yard and playing cornhole. Not that I'm spying.

I just don't know what to do.

One day, Emmie and Bri corner me after art club (and Bri's Science Olympiad meeting).

What's going on, Sarah?

Not that you're the yappiest person, but this isn't like you.

Also, you've barely smiled all week.

What is this, an intervention?

I sigh.

Okay.

We sit down on the stairs and I tell them about Leo.

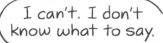
I can't. I don't know what to say.

And I don't want to hurt his feelings.

Sarah... I hate to break it to you...

...but you're doing the exact same thing to Leo that both he and Ben did to you.

You've gotta break the cycle.

I nod slowly. They're right. Of course.
So the next day, I text him.

srry i've been avoiding u. can we talk agn?

...

k. have to finish cleaning room first. but aftr

I wait on my stoop.

After a while, I get kinda irritated that he's taking so long.

Which is a weird realization: I'm not nervous, just impatient.
That's when it hits me.

I can't wait to see him.

This makes me wonder for the first time . . .

Could I ever see Leo as...

I get the "ick" chills and shake it off.
But . . .
Okay, honestly, I don't know if that could ever happen or not.
Only thing I do know right now . . .

Leo *She lost her nerve*

IT'S BEEN A WEEK SINCE SARAH STOPPED TALKING TO ME ... *AGAIN.*

no new messages

this is getting old

AND ABOUT WHAT HAPPENED: EMBARRASSED ISN'T THE WORD.

mortified

humiliated

embarrassed

Wish I could change color and blend into a wall

STILL, I CAN'T STAND NOT
SEEING HER. FEELINGS ASIDE,
I'M REALLY WORRIED WE
WON'T BE FRIENDS ANYMORE.

impossible to believe, like:

unicorns   Bigfoot   non-delicious burgers

THE ONLY THING I HAVE
GOING FOR ME:

Adam   Laney

AN' IT'S NO SMALL THING.
I REALLY LIKE THEM.

I'M EVEN GETTING TO KNOW OTHER KIDS, TOO.

AS FOR BEN, I ADMIT I HAVEN'T EXACTLY BEEN IN TOUCH.

BUT IT'S THE OTHER WAY AROUND, TOO.

GUESS WE FINALLY REALIZE WE DON'T HAVE MUCH IN COMMON ANYMORE.

THE WAY HE TREATED SARAH WAS THE FINAL BLOW.

I'M THINKING ABOUT ALL THIS WHILE DOING STRETCHES NEAR THE BACK FENCE.

Can we talk?

THIS IS IT. THE MOMENT I'VE BEEN HOPING FOR AND DREADING AT THE SAME TIME.

It *was* about 60-40 hope, now it's about 90-10 dread.

gulp

BUT I GUESS THIS NEEDS TO HAPPEN...

...'CAUSE I WANT MY BGF BACK.

SARAH AND LEO

 The (shared) End

He pauses. Then he stands and faces me.

We smile at each other. And I think maybe we have a chance to be friends again.

I go inside, grab what's left of my allowance, and tell my mom where we're going. Leo waits on the stoop.

He kicks a stone down the sidewalk. We watch it bounce a few times and land in a crack.

I stop.

I'm not mad, Leo. I'm happy for you.

Besides, I think it's good for us to have time apart. Makes us happier when we see each other.

 And less annoyed?

 That, too.

giggle

There's something else... I talked to my parents.

(recent) flashback:

 So, wait. You *want* to stay at EW? *Really?* Don't gloat.

Honey, we're not. Despite what you think, we didn't switch you out to be mean.

We did it because you weren't flourishing.

"You were distracted and unfocused."

pfft

Stop, Leo.

We were worried. We thought EW was better suited to your needs.

I laugh, linking arms with him.

I do wonder if things will be weird between us again. I hope not. Even though we agreed to start over, everything is different. Leo admitted his feelings and he can't undo that. It'll always be out there.

But then I glance at him, and he smiles in that Leo way I missed.

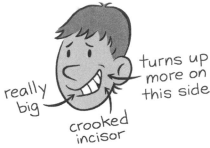

And somehow, like always, I know we'll be okay.

EPILOGUE
SARAH

We walk into Taystee's. It's super crowded. But then, it's Saturday afternoon and about nine thousand degrees out.

I see Joe sitting with Tyler and Anthony. I remember how his dancing helped cheer me up. I wish more people knew what a nice person he is . . .

. . . under all that "class clown" stuff.

Then I see someone else.

Leo notices him, too.
I don't think Ben sees us. He's engrossed in conversation.

probably about Ninja
Robot Assassins III

He doesn't get a chance to answer because it's our turn in line.
We both order Cereal Milk on waffle cones.

After we pay, he glances at Ben.

Who's spotted us.

But we leave anyway, our cones already dripping before we escape the air-conditioning.

Somehow, we make it to my stoop with most of our ice cream intact. We sit and lick our cones (and hands).

As I lick, I feel something bumpy in the ice cream. I pick it out with my fingers and look.

I inspect it.

I look closer.

He pulls something out of his scoop.

We lick our cones silently. I start to daydream about our vast thirteen-year history.

And I think, going forward, whatever decisions we make . . .

. . . whatever crushes we have . . .

. . . and whether we're brave or not about our choices . . .

. . . as long as Leo and I are honest with each other . . .

. . . it'll always work out in the end.

ACKNOWLEDGMENTS

So many people to thank! These books really do take a team and I'm lucky to have the best team behind me.

Lots of thanks to my fabulous editor, Donna Bray. She and I have worked on so many of these books, we now have an enviable flow. I always trust her feedback and ideas, and these stories wouldn't be the same without her.

Also, so much thanks to my incredible agent, Dan Lazar, whose judgment I trust unwaveringly and whose immense support I'm always grateful for.

To Laura Mock and Amy Ryan, total creative superheroes. I so appreciate their talent, enthusiasm, and artistic eye(s).

To Taylan Salvati, Vaishali Nayak, Robert Imfeld, Jon Howard, Gwen Morton, Patty Rosati, and the rest of the hardworking, supportive team at HarperCollins. They raise the bar on excellence.

To my wonderful mom, who gave me so much of her talent and all her perfectionism. Thanks (I think).

To my family: Mike, Mollie, and Nikki. Simply said, you are the best and I am the luckiest. Can't forget the fur baby, Rosie, who I thank for all the stress-cuddles.

Last but not least, I'm eternally grateful to all my readers: without you, these books wouldn't be possible. Keep those main character suggestions coming (Sarah was a clear winner)!

Rosie waiting on her cuddles